# Meg Mackintosh

and

## The Mystery at the
## Soccer Match

A Solve-It-Yourself Mystery

by  Lucinda Landon

Secret Passage Press
Tucker Hollow   North Scituate
Rhode Island

Books by Lucinda Landon
*Meg Mackintosh and the Case of the Missing Babe Ruth Baseball*
*Meg Mackintosh and the Case of the Curious Whale Watch*
*Meg Mackintosh and the Mystery at the Medieval Castle*
*Meg Mackintosh and the Mystery at Camp Creepy*
*Meg Mackintosh and the Mystery in the Locked Library*
*Meg Mackintosh and the Mystery at the Soccer Match*

About the author
*Lucinda Landon has been an avid mystery fan since her childhood.*
*She lives in Rhode Island with her husband, two sons, two dogs,*
*two cats and one horse. Their old house has a secret passage.*

Copyright © 1997 by Lucinda Landon

First Edition

Library of Congress Catalogue Number: 97-068579

ISBN 1-888695-05-6

10 9 8 7 6 5 4 3 2
BP
PRINTED IN THE UNITED STATES OF AMERICA

for Alex Egan

"Go, Hawks!" Meg Mackintosh and her friends cheered their teammates on the soccer field.

"Score!" they yelled excitedly as the Hawks snared a goal.

"We're going to win the gold medal!" Alex and Carmen slapped a high five.

"Meg and Carmen, get ready," Coach Lee called out. "You're going in at the end of this quarter."

"My brother, Peter, is the goalie for the Panthers," Meg told Alex as she tightened her laces. "He's always bragging about how great he is. I wouldn't mind popping a goal past him myself," she said with a smile.

"I wish I had the chance to," said Alex.

"Ooops, sorry, Alex," Meg said, glancing at the cast on his broken leg. "It must be tough sitting out the championship match."

"At least the Hawks are ahead," sighed Alex, hugging his dog. "We've got to win this one, right, Farley?"

Carmen picked up the gold medal on the

trophy table nearby. "I saw a medal like this at a sports museum. It's so heavy, I bet it's solid gold. I'd really love to win it."

"Coach Lee won it playing international soccer a long time ago," Alex told her. "He promised to give it to today's winning team to keep until next year."

"That's great," Meg said. "It must be worth a fortune," she added.

"Yeah, it's great, as long as the Hawks win," Carmen replied.

Their words were nearly drowned out by cheering nearby.

"Come on, Panthers. Heather, get in there and fight!" yelled her dad.

"Sign the soccer petition!" a woman called. "No more awards!"

"Alex, isn't that your Mom?" asked Meg.

"Yes," Alex groaned. "She thinks our soccer league is getting too competitive. She wants to do away with awards."

"No awards?" said Carmen. "How about no yelling," she joked. "The parents are noisier than the kids!"

"My parents are away," said Meg as she scanned the area, "but Gramps and Skip are here — at the hot dog booth, as usual."

Just then the referee's whistle signaled the end of the quarter. It startled Alex's dog, Farley, and he bolted towards the field.

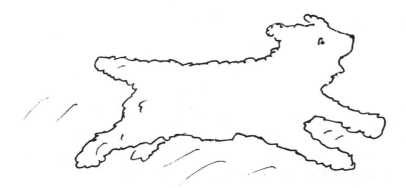

Meg jumped up and caught Farley by his thick fur. He wasn't wearing a collar, so it was hard to hold on. "Sorry, Farley, no dogs allowed in the game!"

Alex hobbled over to retrieve his dog. "I've got him, Meg. Get in there and score!"

Meg gave Alex a thumbs up. "Watch my knapsack, will you? It's got all my detective stuff. Take a look, if you want. I know you're curious about joining our Detective Club."

Alex rolled his eyes at Carmen as he peered into Meg's knapsack. "She really expects a mystery at a soccer match?"

"You know Meg," Carmen answered, as she followed Meg onto the field. "She's always looking for a case to solve."

"Look at the stuff she's got in here," Alex muttered to himself. "Magnifying glass, instant camera, notebook, binoculars, flashlight. There's even a message in code."

He picked up a pencil and started working on the code. "If I could decode the message, I'd really surprise Meg!" he said.

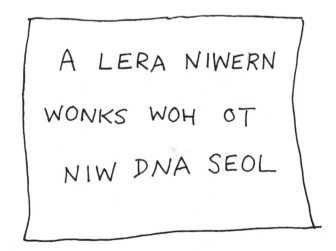

A LERA NIWERN

WONKS WOH OT

NIW DNA SEOL

**CAN YOU CRACK THE CODE?**

Just then it started to
sprinkle, so Alex packed up
Meg's detective kit, except
for her binoculars, which
he used to follow the fancy
footwork on the field.

The Hawks were still on the attack. Meg passed
the ball to Carmen, who drove at the goal, but
Peter and the Panthers turned the ball back. A
moment later, the Panthers scored!

"The Panthers will get that medal yet," Peter
called to Meg. "I can see it now — in my new
display case — on my bureau," he teased.

"Not if I can help it," Meg retorted.

"Come on, Meg," Carmen nudged her. "It's no
use arguing with Peter, especially in front of
everyone."

| HAWKS | 3 | PANTHERS | 2 |

The light rain made the field slippery and a few moments later Peter slid as he reached for the ball. He collided with his teammate Heather, scraping his wrist and her knee.

"Just a bit of skin," Peter said through gritted teeth as he pulled off his bloody goalie glove.

The whistle blew time out and replacements for Peter and Heather ran onto the field. Meg and Carmen were sent back to the sidelines, too.

"Heather," the Panther coach called out. "Get your knee checked out, and get rid of that gum!"

"Oooops," Heather whispered to Peter.

On their way to First Aid, Heather and Peter stopped at the awards table. Meg could just hear their conversation from the sidelines.

"Talk about heavy metal," Peter joked, holding up the award.

"My dad almost won a medal like this a long time ago," Heather told Peter.

Heather's dad joined them. "The Panthers are

sure to win it today," he boasted as he cracked open a peanut. "Now, Heather, you've got to get tough! You want to win that medal, don't you?"

"I don't think they should give out awards. It's not fair for everyone, and feelings get hurt," said Alex's mom. "My petition recommends that neither team receive the gold medal. If it were up to me, I'd get rid of it right now!"

Heather's dad just gave her a funny look. "We should at least cover the table so the awards don't get soaked. I'll go get a blanket from my car," he volunteered.

"I guess I could hold my umbrella over the table until you get back," Alex's mom offered.

"Remember, Heather," her dad told her as he left for the car, "Be sure to ask your coach if you can get right back in the game."

"Okay," said Heather. But once her dad was out of earshot Heather said to Peter, "I don't want to play anymore. But if we don't win the medal, my dad will be really disappointed."

Heather's dad returned with the blanket, and the four of them covered the table. Then the two parents went to watch the game with the other spectators while Heather and Peter went on to First Aid.

16

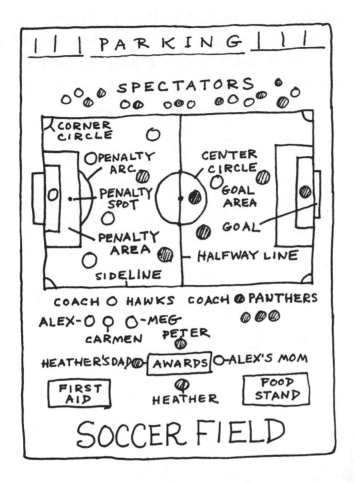

SOCCER FIELD

Meanwhile the Hawks and Panthers crisscrossed the field. When the halftime whistle blew, the two teams returned to the sidelines. The Hawks were still in the lead — but barely.

HAWKS 4 PANTHERS 3

Near the end of the half-time break, the sun came out, and Heather's dad returned to the uncover the awards table. Suddenly he let out a yell that sounded like it came over a loud speaker.

"The gold medal is gone!" he cried.

Meg grabbed her instant camera and rushed to the scene. The famous medal was missing. Its empty case sat in the center of the table. "Just enough rain to leave footprints," Meg observed. She snapped a photo, hoping to preserve any clues, and grabbed her notebook to make a list.

HOW MANY CLUES CAN
YOU FIND IN MEG'S PHOTO?

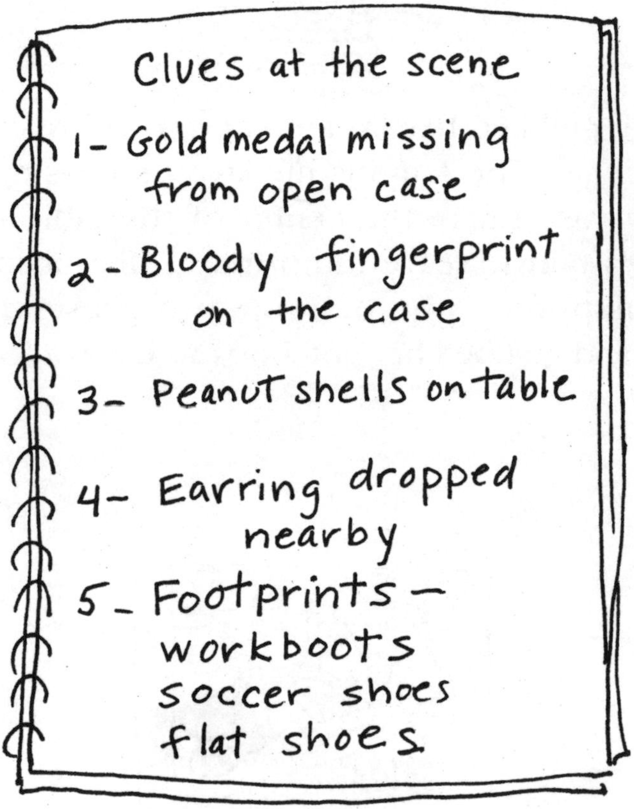

Clues at the scene
1- Gold medal missing
    from open case

2- Bloody fingerprint
    on the case

3- Peanut shells on table

4- Earring dropped
    nearby

5- Footprints —
    workboots
    soccer shoes
    flat shoes.

Meg looked up from her notebook and turned to Alex's mom. "When was the last time you saw the medal?" she asked.

20

"I'm sure it was there when we covered the table. I think the case was open. Maybe the medal just fell out." Alex's mom bit her lip. "It's got to be here somewhere."

"I didn't see it, but I did find this earring," Meg replied. "It looks like it's yours."

"It *is* mine. I didn't even know I'd lost it!" Alex's mom seemed flustered.

Meg leaned over the table and examined the case, careful not to touch it. "It looks like there are fingerprints on the case," she said. "Lots of them. How many people touched it?" she asked.

WHO COULD HAVE PICKED UP THE MEDAL?

"I picked it up," Carmen said. "Hey, Peter, you have a cut," she shot him a glance. "That could be your bloody fingerprint."

"I did pick it up," replied Peter. "But I didn't take it!"

"I picked it up, too," said Heather. "I was checking the date."

"I looked at it, to make sure it was authentic," admitted Heather's dad. "This is so unfair that it was stolen! Now what will the Panthers get for a prize?"

"I glanced at it, too" said Alex's mom nervously. "They aren't going to fingerprint us, are they?""

"Mom, take it easy. It sounds like just about everybody touched it," said Alex.

"Do you think we should call the police?" Carmen asked.

"If it isn't found by the end of the match, I may have to," Coach Lee replied sadly.

"Now is my chance to really score," Meg said to herself. "Maybe I can solve this mystery before they call the police!"

"Parents, please. I'm sure there's a very reasonable explanation," said the referee, then she blew her whistle. "Half time's over — now let's play soccer!"

"Meg, you don't suspect my mother, do you?" asked Alex.

"Not in particular," Meg said. "But everyone who was around the table is a suspect," she added. "They all picked up the medal at one time or another."

"Come on, Meg." said Carmen. "You'll have to solve this later. We've got to play."

"I guess you're right," Meg said reluctantly. She thought for a moment, then tossed her knapsack to Alex. "Okay Alex, now *you're* the detective. If you want to join the Detective Club, help me solve the case."

"H-h-how?" stammered Alex. "I don't know what to do!"

"Don't worry," said Meg. "I made a chart to help you get started."

| suspects | motives | clues |
|---|---|---|
| Heather | | |
| Heather's Dad | | |
| Peter | | |
| Alex's Mom | | |
| Others- | | |

"It's hard to suspect friends and relatives," Meg said. "I know — for instance, it could have been my brother. But you have to look at the evidence with an open mind."

WHAT ARE THE POSSIBLE MOTIVES AND EVIDENCE FOR EACH OF THE SUSPECTS?

Alex started filling in the chart, but his attention was mostly on the field. The Hawks started to slip: they couldn't get a goal past Peter, and then the Panthers scored, tying the match 4 - 4.

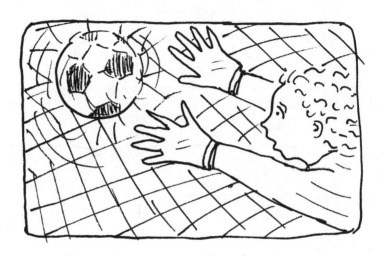

At the end of the third quarter, Meg and Carmen were side-lined again.

"Let's see what you've got," Meg said, reaching for Alex's notes. "Hey! You think Carmen and I are suspects?" she added.

Alex grinned. "You said that everyone who was near the table at the end of half-time was a suspect. And everybody heard you and Peter arguing about wanting the medal."

"Fair enough," said Meg. "The problem is, everyone is a suspect — but we really don't have enough substantial evidence against anyone."

She renewed Alex's notes and added a few of her own.

| Suspects | Motives | Clues |
|---|---|---|
| Heather | Dad really wants her to win the medal | soccer footprint |
| Heather's Dad | He almost won a medal like the one stolen | dropped peanut shells |
| Peter | bragged about new case for medal | bloody fingerprint |
| Alex's Mom | doesn't like awards! | lost her earring |
| Others— Meg + Carmen | Both said the medal worth a fortune Meg argued with Peter | Both were near the table |

Meg bit her thumbnail, then flipped to the next page in her notebook. "Time to switch tactics. If I can't figure out *who* took the medal, I'll concentrate on *where* the thief could have hidden it."

### WHERE COULD THE MEDAL POSSIBLY BE HIDDEN?

"When in doubt. . .doodle" Meg said to herself. "If I brainstorm long enough, a good idea might surface."

"Score!" yelled the crowd.

"Oh, no!" Alex cried.

Meg looked up. It was the Panthers scoring, not the Hawks! She tried to focus on the case.

HAWKS | 4 | PANTHERS | 5

"Did you take any instant photos?" Meg asked Alex. "Maybe looking at them will help the investigation."

"Just a couple," said Alex, pulling them out of his pocket.

"Some nice portraits of Farley," Meg said with a bit of disappointment.

She'd hardly had a chance to look at them when Coach Lee called out, "Meg, Carmen, you're going back in there!"

"Maybe I'll spy something out on the field," Meg said to Alex. She handed him her notebook and binoculars and raced back into the match.

The Hawks were playing hard, but the Panthers were relentless. Peter rescued every goal attempt and punted the ball back to his teammates.

"Look who's smiling now, Meg-O," Peter grinned. "The medal is ours!"

"It's not over yet," Meg said firmly. "And we'll have to *find* the medal first — unless you already know where it is."

Peter just gave her a funny look.

A few minutes later, the Panthers scored again. Over on the sidelines Alex groaned, "I can't watch anymore." He scanned the area. "Where's Farley?" he wondered.

HAWKS | 4 | PANTHERS | 6

Meanwhile, Meg got control of the ball and blasted towards the goal. She passed it to Carmen, who passed it back. Then, with a magnificent kick, Meg sent the ball over Peter's head and into the corner of the net.

"Yeah, Meg!" cheered the Hawks.

But it wasn't enough. Before the Hawks could score again, the final whistle blew.

"Good game, everyone" said Coach Lee. "We did our best and worked hard. That's what counts."

HAWKS | 5 | PANTHERS | 6

"I wish we'd won," said Carmen. "But we still wouldn't get the medal. I'm going to find my parents. I'll catch up with you later."

"I want to find it anyway," said Meg. She looked at Alex. "Any developments?"

"As a matter of fact, I found an important clue," Alex answered. He pulled a small piece of paper from his pocket. "I found this next to the medal's case and if you ask me, it points straight to the culprit."

Meg's jaw dropped.

WHO DOES THE CLUE POINT TO?

"A bubble gum wrapper," said Meg. "But what does that prove? Anybody can chew gum."

"True," said Alex, "but Heather is *always* chewing bubble gum. I saw her blow a big bubble right after she and Peter collided in the first half. *And* remember this photo I took of her and Farley while she was on the sidelines."

Meg shook her head. "It's just not hard evidence. All it proves is that Heather was at the table, not that she stole something from it."

"Well, I have a hunch," said Alex. "Come on, I'll prove it."

Meg studied the photo, then followed Alex curiously. "Maybe he's a better detective than I thought," she said to herself. "I think his hunch could be right."

Alex led Meg up to Heather. "Congratulations on

winning the match. It's too bad we can't find the prize medal," he said.

"Yeah," said Heather. "Maybe it will turn up."

"Maybe the player who took it will give it back," said Alex.

"What do you mean?" said Heather. She couldn't look Alex in the face. Her own face turned bright red.

"I think you know what I mean," said Alex. "Why don't you just give it up now?"

HEATHER

"I don't have it, honest!" cried Heather.

"She's telling the truth," Peter butted in. "She doesn't have it."

"How can you be sure?" asked Alex. "Unless you took it yourself, that is!"

"No, really ... I ... " Peter trailed off.

"Peter, what's going on?" Meg glared at him. "You'd better explain — fast."

"Alex is right about one thing — Heather *did* take the medal. I saw her hiding it," Peter said. "But I talked her into returning it and I saw her put it back."

"I saw where she hid it, too," agreed Meg.

WHERE DID HEATHER HIDE
THE MEDAL?

"You put it in your shinguard!" exclaimed Meg. "There's the tip of the striped ribbon showing near your knee in the photo!"

"I'm sorry," Heather cried. "I wanted to win so much. It was wrong and so stupid. I hid the medal in my shinguard while Peter and I were at First Aid. But I felt bad about taking it," she sobbed. "I put it back just a little while ago."

"Heather, you'd better explain this to the others," said Meg.

"Go on, tell them." Peter nudged Heather as people gathered around the table.

"Did you find it?" asked Heather's dad.

Heather hesitated. "It should be right here; I put it back in the case." She snapped it open.

"What happened? It's not here!" Heather began to cry. "I did put the medal back, honest."

"HEATHER! I can't believe you'd steal something!" Heather's dad acted shocked.

"Maybe she felt that she had to," Carmen muttered under her breath. "Her dad's pretty pushy."

"I bet she still has it," said Alex.

"But why would she lie about it now?" wondered Meg as she took another photograph of the awards table. She compared it to the first photograph of the scene and jotted down the differences.

HALF-TIME

END OF GAME

**WHAT DIFFERENCES DID MEG NOTICE?**

Differences between
the two photos
1 - Case is shut - it
   was open before
2 - Peanut shells have
   been cleaned up
3 - Earring has been
   returned
4 - Footprints -
   soccer shoe
   dog prints
   mysterious round one

"Don't look so glum, Meg-O," said Peter. "You played a good game — the Hawks were doing great until the second half."

"I'm not sad about losing. You deserved to win," said Meg. "I just want to figure out what happened to the gold medal. Did Heather put the it back because she realized the Panthers were going to win it anyway?"

"No, honest, she said she was putting it back no matter what." Peter noticed a piece of paper next to Meg's knapsack. "Hey, here's that secret message. Give me your pencil and I'll finish it up."

Meg fumbled in her knapsack. "Can't find it," she said and handed him her pen instead. "You're pretty smart, do the puzzle in ink!"

"Gee, thanks," joked Peter.

But Meg wasn't listening. Suddenly she realized she had missed two important clues. She grabbed her magnifying glass and examined her photos again. "Just as I thought!" she said. "Something that *should* be in the first photo isn't there, and something that *shouldn't* be in the second photo is!"

WHAT CLUES HAD MEG MISSED?

HALF-TIME

END O

"Why isn't the gum wrapper in the first photo?" Meg wondered out loud. "And what's my pencil doing in the second one? That's why you have to solve the code in ink!"

"How can you be sure it's your pencil?" asked Peter.

"It's got my teethmarks on it!" But before Meg could explain further, two paws landed on her notebook. It was her dog, Skip. She had been taking Gramps for a walk around the soccer field.

"Good match, kids," Gramps said. "Too bad you both couldn't win. But then you would have to tie, or be on the same team, or some such. Oh, never mind. Hand me your camera and I'll take your picture."

"Cheesedoodles," Meg and Peter chorused, smiling as Gramps clicked the shutter.

Suddenly Skip yanked her leash out of Gramps's hand and charged off to play with Farley.

"Come on, girl" Meg called. She caught up to the dogs and grabbed them both by their collars — one in each hand.

"Hold on, I'll take a photo of the pups, too," Gramps said.

"What about the mystery, Meg-O," Peter reminded her. "You said there were two things about the photos that were odd — what else?"

"Actually, there are four careless clues," said Meg, as she watched the instant photos develop.

WHAT ARE THE FOUR CARELESS CLUES?

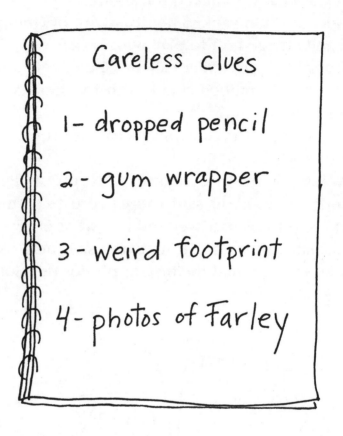

Careless clues

1 - dropped pencil

2 - gum wrapper

3 - weird footprint

4 - photos of Farley

"I'll explain in a minute," Meg told Peter as she re-examined her notes and photos.

"But first, it's time to award the gold medal," said Meg.

"What do you mean? It's missing," Peter said.

"Not anymore," Meg answered. "I just figured out who took it, why, and where they put it." Meg snapped her notebook shut and pointed. "It's someone standing over there."

**WHO TOOK THE GOLD MEDAL?**

"Hey Alex!" Meg took him aside. "You really caught on to detective work fast."

"I guess I *am* pretty good at it." Alex said, blushing.

"But you don't fool me — anymore," she continued.

"What do you mean?" he stammered.

"I bet you knew that Heather took the medal, because you *saw* her put it back at the end of the game. Then, you decided to take it yourself — so you planted a clue that would make Heather look guilty."

"You put the gum wrapper on the award table," Meg continued. "You figured everyone would think it was Heather's. But if she *had* dropped it when she took the medal, it would have been at the scene of the crime all along."

"How do you know it wasn't there, Meg," Alex asked.

"It isn't in the first photo I took of the scene," Meg answered.

Alex looked around nervously. "It's still not proof that I had anything to do with the missing medal," he argued.

"By itself it's not," Meg agreed. "But it helped me pick up on other clues — including one that shows where you hid the medal. Look at this picture," she said, pulling out the ones Gramps had taken only moments before, along with one Alex had taken earlier."

"I don't know what you're talking about — I don't have it." Alex shrugged his shoulders.

"It's no use, Alex. You left so many careless clues, and I know where you hid the medal."

WHERE IS THE GOLD MEDAL ?

Meg whistled for Farley and pulled his collar over his head. Because of Farley's thick fur it looked like a regular dog collar, but it was the gold medal!

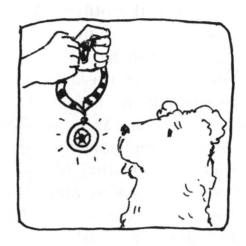

"Sharp eyes, Meg-O!" Peter exclaimed

"That wasn't the only clue," Meg replied. "When I caught Farley early in the game, I had to hang on to his fur, because he didn't have a collar. But when I went to grab him a few minutes ago, he *did* have a collar."

"What about the pencil?" Peter asked again.

"It wasn't in the first crime scene photo, but it was in the second," Meg answered. "I knew Alex had been using it on my word puzzle, so I figured he dropped it at the scene by accident. And I figured out what the strange round footprint was in the mud — the print from Alex's cast!"

"You're right," Alex confessed, kicking the dirt hard with his cast. "I couldn't stand to let the Panthers have the medal. When I saw Heather put it back, it seemed the perfect chance to get it."

Alex hung his head. "Sorry, Meg."

"Don't tell me, tell the others. Go give it to Coach Lee and tell him the truth."

"What do you think Heather's and Alex's punishment will be?" Peter asked Meg after Alex left to talk to Coach Lee.

"It's hard to say," said Meg. "Admitting that you're wrong isn't always enough."

"Maybe if Alex and Heather had unscrambled the secret message, they would have thought twice," Peter said.

"You mean you solved it?" asked Meg.

"Sure thing," Peter said. "A real . . .

A ~~LERA~~ ~~NIWERN~~
A REAL WINNER
~~WONKS~~ ~~WOH~~ ~~OT~~
KNOWS HOW TO
~~NIW~~ ~~DNA~~ ~~SEOL~~
WIN AND LOSE

"... winner knows how to win and lose," he read.

"You can say that again," said Meg.

And so, of course, he did.